Fireman Sam ™

THIS ANNUAL BELONGS TO

·····································

EGMONT
We bring stories to life

First published in Great Britain 2011
by Egmont UK Limited,
239 Kensington High Street, London W8 6SA

Text by Catherine Shoolbred. Design by Oscar Spigolon
and Kate Grove.

© 2011 Prism Art & Design Limited, a HIT Entertainment company.
Based on an original idea by D. Gingell, D. Jones and original
characters created by R. M. J. Lee.

ISBN 978 1 4052 5811 1
10 9 8 7 6 5 4 3 2 1
Printed in Italy

Adult supervision is recommended when glue, paint, scissors and
other sharp points are in use.

CONTENTS

MEET SAM AND THE RESCUE CREW!

FIREMAN SAM

Fireman Sam is the **hero** next door! He is brave, kind and always ready to drive **Jupiter** to the rescue.

PENNY

Penny helps the team to tackle fires. She drives **Venus** the rescue tender and uses **Neptune** for emergencies at sea.

COLOUR

Neptune bright yellow, so it's ready to rescue!

ELVIS, STATION OFFICER STEELE AND RADAR

Station Officer Steele runs the Pontypandy **Fire Station**. Elvis is a **firefighter** and the station cook. Radar is a trained **rescue dog**.

TOM

Tom Thomas leads **mountain rescues**. He flies the rescue helicopter, **Wallaby One**.

COLOUR
Tom Thomas' rescue outfit bright orange.

MEET THEIR FRIENDS!

DILYS AND NORMAN

Dilys Price runs the **local shop.** Her son Norman is always in trouble, so he's known as **Naughty Norman!**

COLOUR
Norman and his friend Woolly, so they can play!

MIKE, HELEN AND MANDY

Mike Flood is always having **accidents,** but luckily he's married to **Nurse Helen!** Mandy is Norman's **best friend,** so she's often in trouble, too!

CHARLIE, BRONWYN, JAMES AND SARAH

Charlie Jones is a **fisherman** married to Bronwyn. Their **twins**, James and Sarah, like exploring. When James grows up, he wants to be a **fireman** just like Sam!

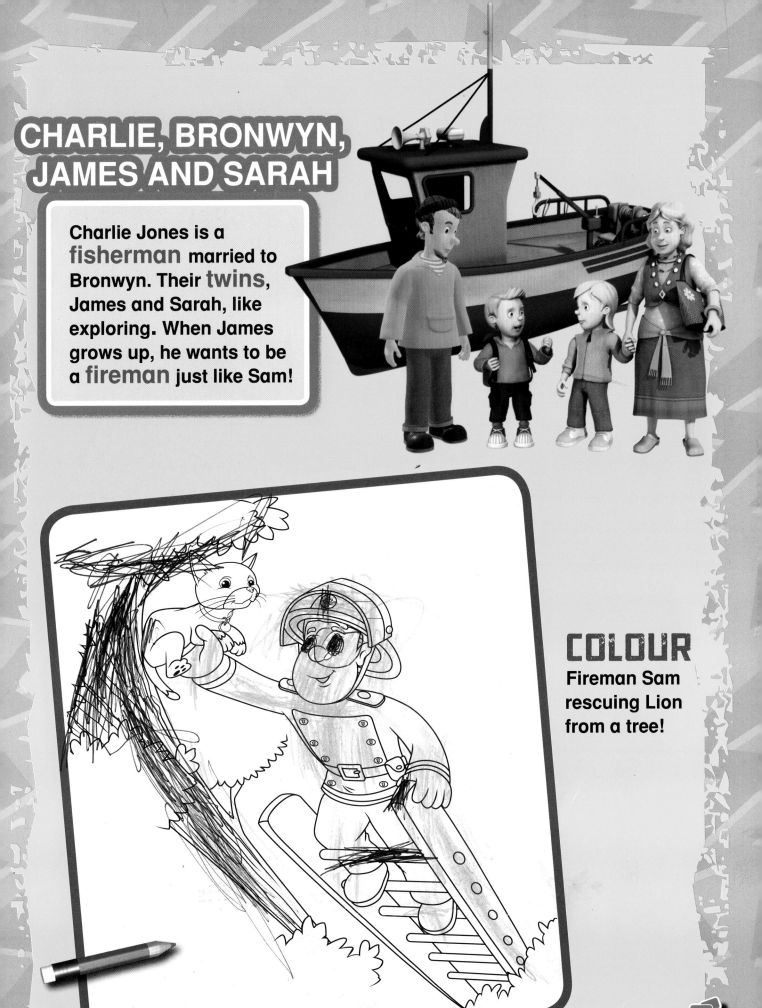

COLOUR

Fireman Sam rescuing Lion from a tree!

FIREMAN JAMES

The fire crew are checking the Pontypandy fire hydrants, to make sure they have plenty of water to put out fires ...

The team uses Jupiter's radio to stay in touch with the fire station.

"You can be the radio man today, Elvis!" Sam says.

"Yesss!" replies Elvis, excitedly.

Nee Nah, Nee Nah!

Fire fighters to the rescue!

Charlie and Sarah pretend to be firefighters with their walkie-talkies.

"Quick, Fireman James, put out the fire!" says Sarah.

"This is fun, but it would better if I was a REAL fireman like Fireman Sam," says James.

Then, to their amazement, they hear Station Officer Steele's voice through their walkie-talkie!

"Base to Jupiter," he says.

James and Sarah can't believe it!

"Jupiter, where ARE you?" repeats Station Officer Steele.

"Oooh, my first radio call!" says Elvis. "Um … Hello. Is everything OK?"

"No Cridlington, that's why I'm calling! Lion is locked in Mike's van on the High Street! Go and rescue his keys from the drain."

Fireman James to the rescue!

13

Meeeooooww!

Nee Nah, Nee Nah!

"Help is on the way!" Mike tells Lion. But before Jupiter gets there, James arrives.

"I can get your keys with my magnet," he tells Mike.

James lowers his magnet into the drain. When he lifts it back up, Mike's keys are attached.

"Nice one, Fireman James!" says Mike, as he gets Lion.

When the crew arrives, Mike tells them what James has done.

"Good work, Fireman James," says Sam.

"One day I want to be a real fireman just like you!" James tells him.

"I'm sure you will be!" Sam replies.

14

As the crew checks the last hydrant, their radio crackles into life:

"Base to Jupiter. Norman is stuck up a tree on Hibbert Street."

Back in town, James hears the call and goes to fetch his dad's ladder.

Help!

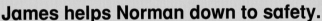
James helps Norman down to safety.

"You beat us again!" Sam says, when he arrives. "But do be careful, some rescues need to be done by trained professionals."

Later, Mike's cooker catches fire! Station Officer Steele puts out the rescue call to Jupiter, but James also rushes to help.

Mike doesn't see James go into his house. It fills with smoke, and James is soon lost in the dark.

Mike realises James is in the house! Sam and Elvis put on breathing equipment and hurry inside.

Elvis turns off the power and puts out the fire, while Sam looks for James.

"Take my hand," Sam says, as he guides James to safety.

"Hooray!" shouts Sarah, when Sam comes out with James.

"And the fire's out, too!" smiles Elvis.

I'll lead you out!

"I won't listen to my walkie-talkie again!" says James.

"So that's how you got there first, you picked up our radio signals," says Sam.

"I'm sorry, I wanted to be a fireman but I don't think I do anymore!" James replies.

"Don't be hasty, you could be a good fireman one day," Sam tells him.

"But you need training first," smiles Penny.

"I can teach you how to use the radio!" says Elvis.

Suddenly, Jupiter's radio crackles into life: "Base calling Cridlington. Where are you?"

"Hello?" Elvis says, looking all around for Station Officer Steele. "Oops, he's on the radio!" he blushes, as he rushes to answer it.

Everyone giggles behind him!

THE END

EMERGENCY CALL!

Trace the red line to see who Officer Steele sends to a mountain rescue. Then follow the blue line to see who they call and lastly the green line to see who else helps them.

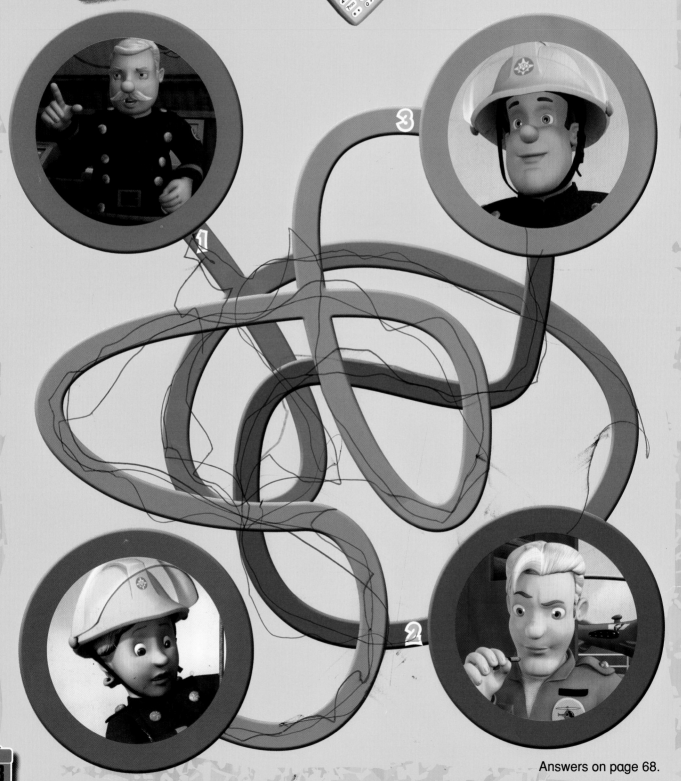

Answers on page 68.

PONTYPANDY PATTERNS

Help Norman complete these patterns, by colouring in the picture at the end of each line.

ODD NORMAN OUT

One of these pictures of Norman skateboarding is different from the others. Can you spot which one?

a

b

c

d

e

Answer on page 68.

PICTURE PERFECT

The fire team's racing into action! Can you spot which one of the below close-ups can't be found in the big picture?

a

b

c

d

e

Answer on page 68.

SAILOR STEELE

Help read this story. Listen to the words and when you see a picture, say the name out loud!

STATION OFFICER STEELE

CHARLIE

FIREMAN SAM

PENNY

ZZ

 is a volunteer firefighter. He is

learning to help  and the team with

fire emergencies. One day, 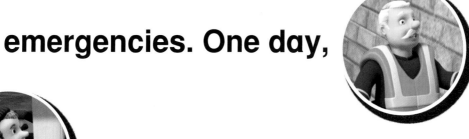 helps

 catch fish for the café. He pretends

that he knows all about boats, but he forgets

to tie the lobster pots to

the boat and gets

pinched by a crab!

 drops the crab back into the sea.

"Shame," says . "It was a big one."

"What shall we do now?"  asks.

"We fish!" replies , as he gives him

a fishing rod. "Aye, aye, Sir!" says .

They don't catch any fish all afternoon, so

they decide to go home.  spills

some petrol as he fills the engine and when

he turns it on, a fire starts. "Fire!" yells

  calmly moves the

petrol can away and gives  a fire

extinguisher. "Point it at the base of the fire,"

 tells him. The fire goes out.

The engine is burnt out.  calls the fire station for help. Suddenly, feels a tug on his fishing line – he's caught a fish!

meets at the harbour.

They launch Neptune and race to the rescue.

"So, what happened?"  asks them.

" might not be the best sailor in the

world,"  replies, "but he was great

in a crisis!" "And he caught a fish!"

says. "Yes, he did,"  replies, "and

it's big enough to share, so let's all enjoy it

at the café!"

SEA RESCUE COLOURING

Penny is off for a sea rescue. Colour her in using the colour code.

DRIVING TIME

Follow the lines and write the letters in the boxes to see which rescue vehicle Penny is driving. Then tick your favourite below.

T U N E P N E

Answer on page 68.

27

ARE YOU AN EMERGENCY HERO?

Do you know how to stay safe? Add a tick (✔) by the things you should do and a cross (✗) by the ones you shouldn't do!

SAM'S TOP TIP:
NEVER play with matches. They start fires and put you in danger!

1 Should you watch food as it cooks?

2 Should you test your smoke alarm?

3 Should you burn candles near curtains?

IF THERE IS A FIRE ...

4 Should you get out of the house?

5 Should you stop to get your valuables?

6 Should you phone 999?

HOW DID YOU DO? Turn to page 68 and give yourself 1 point for every ✔ and ✗ you get right. See opposite for why these things are important ...

DID YOU KNOW...?

If food gets too hot, it can catch fire. Adults should turn the cooker down or off if they leave the kitchen.

Smoke alarms sense smoke before you can. Test them regularly to check if the batteries need to be replaced.

Candles can burn curtains! Adults must blow them out if they leave the room.

IF THERE IS A FIRE ...

Don't stop to get your valuables, they can be replaced.

Leave the house immediately so you are safe.

Call 999 and ask for the fire service. Give them your address so they can help as quickly as possible.

Meanwhile, Elvis lowers a hook into the plughole.

Right a bit, that's it.

Now bring the hook up slowly.

Got it! Now let me at that cake!

Oh no, that's not a flower!

Derek thinks he spots a flower by the cliff, but it's a bit of red paper. Suddenly the cliff edge gives way ...

... Derek falls over the edge. He's stuck!

OOH, HEEELP!!!

Back at the house, Norman finds joke toys in Derek's suitcase. He's just like Norman!

I hope he's back soon, so we can play with all this stuff.

But what if Derek's in danger? I'd better get mum to call Fireman Sam, he'll know what to do!

The crew is about to eat some cake when the alarm sounds. "Derek Price is lost on the mountain. Norman thinks he knows where, so take him with you," Officer Steele tells them.

Sorry, Elvis, your cake will have to wait!

Norman sets off with Sam and Elvis.

He shows them where he told Derek to go.

He must be close by. Let's turn off the siren in case he's calling for help.

As they pass the cliff, they hear a faint voice ...

That's him! He's fallen over the cliff!

The ledge is unstable. We need to get him quickly!

Sam puts on a safety harness.

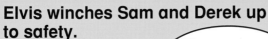

There we are, safe and sound.

I'm sorry I tricked you, Derek. I wanted mum to think I'm her only treasure.

That's OK, I understand. Shake hands?

Let's get you two jokers home.

Oooh! Cool, you have a hand buzzer!

BZZZ!

Then we can eat my cake!

But back at the station ...

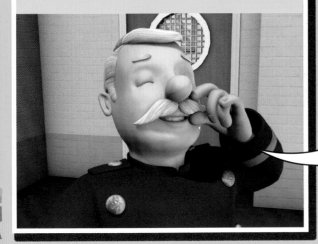

Thanks for leaving the cake for me. I've managed to eat every last chocolate mouthful!

Oh, no!

THE END

RED FOR DANGER!

Sing Elvis' song, then look at all these red things!

*Red is for danger,
Red is what I said.
So if you're in danger,
The colour is red!*

Warning signs are shown in red triangles. This one tells people that a path is dangerous.

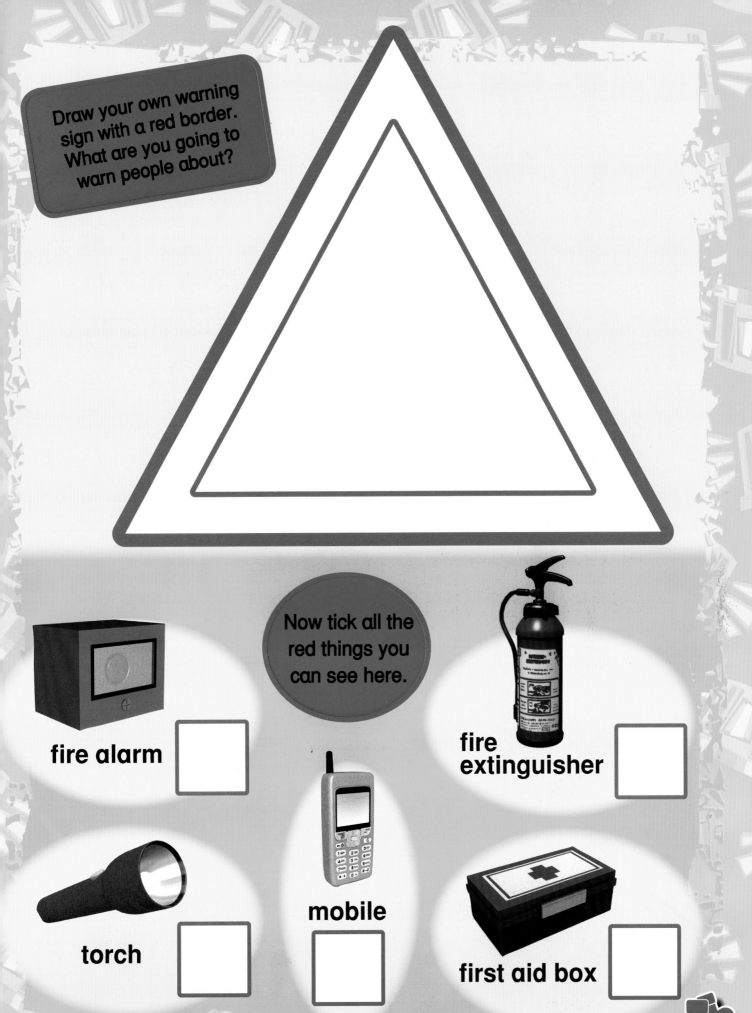

Draw your own warning sign with a red border. What are you going to warn people about?

Now tick all the red things you can see here.

fire alarm

fire extinguisher

torch

mobile

first aid box

Answers on page 68.

MAKE SAM'S FIRE STATION

Ask an adult to photocopy this page and glue it onto card. Cut out Sam and the semicircle and slot them together. Then make his fire station!

WHAT YOU NEED:
- LARGE CARDBOARD BOX
- CARD SHEET
- BLACK PEN
- RED, YELLOW, BROWN, BLACK AND WHITE PAINTS
- GLUE
- SMALL STICK
- CHILD-SAFE SCISSORS

FIRE STATION

WHAT TO DO ...

1 Find a cardboard box big enough for your toys to be able to go out through doors on the front. Paint the box brown and then leave it to dry.

2 Paint the sides of the box yellow, then add 2 yellow rectangles for the windows and 2 for the doors and let it dry.

3 Use the black pen and grey paint to add detail on the windows and doors. Paint the doors red and when dry, cut around them so they can open.

FIRE STATION

STATION FLAG
Glue the flag onto a small stick. Then ask an adult to attach it to the station roof.

STATION CLOCK
Draw on the clock hands then stick it on the station as shown. Now you're ready for action!

41

HEAP OF TROUBLE

It's the day of the Pontypandy Flower and Vegetable Show. Will it all go to plan?

Station Officer Steele shows Elvis his tomato plant.

"As Sam's the judge, he shouldn't see it yet. Can you take it to Mike's house?" he asks.

"Of course I can," Elvis replies.

Mike has grown a marrow on his compost heap for the competition.

Don't forgot to dig over your compost heap. The rotten peelings heat up and could catch fire!

Did you hear that, Dad?

Yes, I'll do it after I pick the marrow.

When Mike takes his marrow off the compost heap, it leaves a big hole in the heap.

Not now, Mandy, it's nearly time for the show to start!

Are you going to dig over the heap like Sam said?

Everyone brings plants for the competition. Elvis hides the damaged tomato plant behind Dilys' plastic flowers.

Where is my plant, Elvis?

Erm, I've put it in the shade so it doesn't dry out.

Good idea, Cridlington!

Bronwyn and the twins arrive just in time with their mustard and cress plants. But then disaster strikes ...

Oh, no!

... the compost heap is on fire!

Quick, call the fire station!

Sam and Penny rush to the Floods' house.

They pour water into the hole on the compost heap to put out the fire.

The twins' plants win the competition. Sam also gives a prize for the funniest plant – the broken tomato plant. Everyone laughs, even Station Officer Steele!

THE END

ODD ONES OUT

Sam needs your help! Can you spot the odd one out in each row?

a

b

c

d

a

b

c

d

a

b

c

d

a

b

c

d

48

Answers on page 68.

ELVIS DOT-TO-DOT

Starting at number 1, join the dots to complete this picture of Elvis and colour him in. Then draw a tasty cake for him to enjoy!

Draw a cake here!

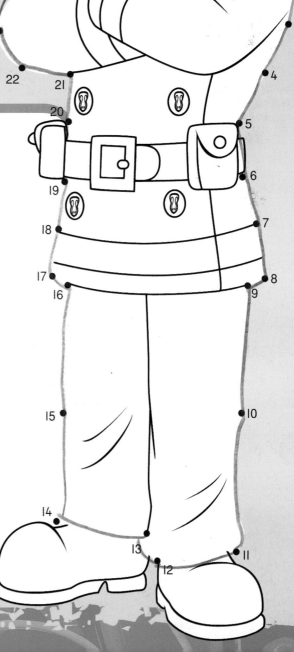

POLES AND LADDERS

Join Sam and the team as you go up the ladders and down the poles in this game!

POORLY PENNY

Help read this story. Listen to the words and when you see a picture, say the name out loud!

PENNY

FIREMAN SAM

CHARLIE

JAMES

LION

SARAH

Atishoo!

 and  enjoy a barbecue

on Pontypandy beach with their parents.

Afterwards,  and  look

for . Where has he gone?

Suddenly,  spots  on the boathouse roof!  doesn't feel well, but she comes out to rescue .  sneezes loudly, **Atishoo!**, as she lifts  off the high roof.

Not long after  gets back to the

station,  calls her out again when

he accidentally sets a bin on fire!

has the day off, but he hears Jupiter's siren

and wonders what he is missing.

 takes his family out fishing.

They don't catch any fish, but

gets his line caught on a buoy, which gets

pulled into the boat's propeller. The boat

is stuck!  comes to the rescue,

but she feels too ill to help them.

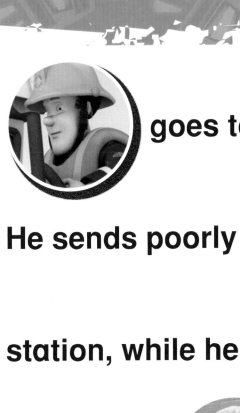 goes to help with the rescue.

He sends poorly  to rest at the

station, while he rescues  and

his family.  is sorry that

had to work on his day off, but

agrees it's hard to stay away from the best

job in the world!

THE
END

SPOT THE DIFFERENCE

These team photos look the same. Can you spot 6 changes in picture 2?

Say cheese!

58

2

Colour in a flame as you spot each change.

STRANDED!

Mandy is playing with Norman at the beach when she finds someone very unusual who needs rescuing!

"You won't find anything as good as I can on the beach!" Norman brags.

"We'll see!" Mandy replies, as she walks away.

When Mandy passes a big rock, she sees a baby whale on the beach!

Wow, a whale!

At the fire station, Trevor is taking a team photo. He clicks the camera button, but nothing happens. "Sorry, I forgot to put film in!" he says. "Stay where you are, this won't take a minute!"

Whoops!

I'll help you!

"I've found a baby whale, I'm going for help!" Mandy shouts to Norman. "Yeah and I've found a mermaid!" Norman jokes to himself.

"It must have been washed up by the high tide," Charlie tells Mandy. "I'll call Sam, but we must keep it wet until it is back in the water."

Trevor's ready to take the photo again when the alarm goes. Sam, Elvis and Penny rush to the beach. Trevor takes photos of Station Officer Steele until they return.

The crew pumps seawater over the whale. "How are we going to get him back into the sea?" Charlie asks Sam. "We'll need Neptune and Wallaby One," Sam tells them, as he gets out his phone.

Click! Click! Click! Back at the station, Trevor takes lots of pictures. Officer Steele poses with a hose and even slides down the pole!

Tom's helicopter hovers over the beach. A harness is wrapped around the whale, then the helicopter slowly lifts it into the sky.

Sam gives Mandy a life jacket, so she can join him on Neptune.

The whale is slowly lowered into the ocean.

Mandy watches as the whale swims over to his mother.

Will he be OK?

He will now he's back where he belongs!

Finally everyone's back for the team photo.
"At last, a proper photo of the Pontypandy Fire Brigade!"
Officer Steele says proudly.
Trevor clicks the button, then lowers his camera. "I'm so
sorry," he says. "I, erm, appear to have run out of film."

"What have you been taking pictures of?" Sam asks.
"Well, I took lots of ..." begins Trevor, looking at
Officer Steele. "Erm, is that the phone?" Officer
Steele says, hurrying away. They'll have to do the
team photo another day!

COUNTING RESCUE VEHICLES

Sam and the Pontypandy rescue crew drive many vehicles during rescues. Count how many you can see of each and write the numbers in the boxes below.

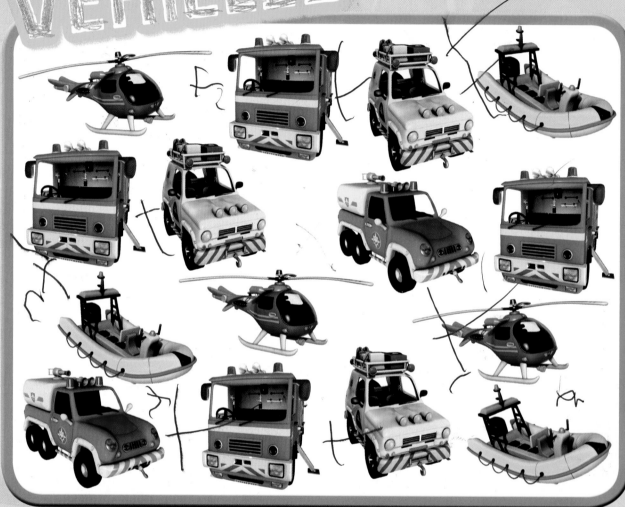

Jupiter

Venus

Wallaby One

Rescue Jeep

Neptune

Jupiter	Venus	Wallaby One	Rescue Jeep	Neptune
4	2	3	3	3

Answers on page 68.

FIRE DASH

Sam needs to put out lots of fires on his way to the fire station. Help him by counting the fires along the way.

Start

Finish

There are

9

fires

Answer on page 68.

ANSWERS

Page 18 EMERGENCY CALL!
Tom Thomas is sent on a mountain rescue. Tom calls Fireman Sam, and Penny also helps them.

Page 20 ODD NORMAN OUT

Page 21 PICTURE PERFECT
Image c can't be found in the big picture.

Page 29 DRIVING TIME
Penny is driving Neptune.

Page 30 ARE YOU AN EMERGENCY HERO?
1 : ✔, 2 : ✔, 3 : ✘,

4 : ✔, 5 : ✘ , 6 : ✔

SCORING:
1-3 correct = You're a Trainee Hero.
4-6 correct = Are you Fireman Sam?

Page 39 RED FOR DANGER

Page 48 ODD ONES OUT
The odd ones out are: Radar = b, Fireman Sam = d, Norman = a, Tom = c.

Page 58 SPOT THE DIFFERENCE

Page 66 COUNTING RESCUE VEHICLES
Jupiter = 4, Venus = 2, Wallaby One = 3, Rescue Jeep = 3 and Neptune = 3.

Page 67 FIRE DASH
There are 9 fires for Sam to put out.